THIS BOOK
BELONGS TO:

SCHOOL PLAY

ASSEMBLY HALL, 4:30 PM
LAST DAY OF THE SEMESTER

To Mum, Blog, and Charlotte

—HW

little bee books

New York, NY
Text and Art Copyright © 2022 by Harry Woodgate
All rights reserved, including the right of reproduction
in whole or in part in any form.
Manufactured in China TPL 0222
First Edition
10 9 8 7 6 5 4 3 2 1
Library of Congress Cataloging-in-Publication Data
is available upon request.
ISBN 978-1-4998-1305-0
littlebeebooks.com
For information about special discounts
on bulk purchases, please contact Little Bee Books
at sales@littlebeebooks.com.

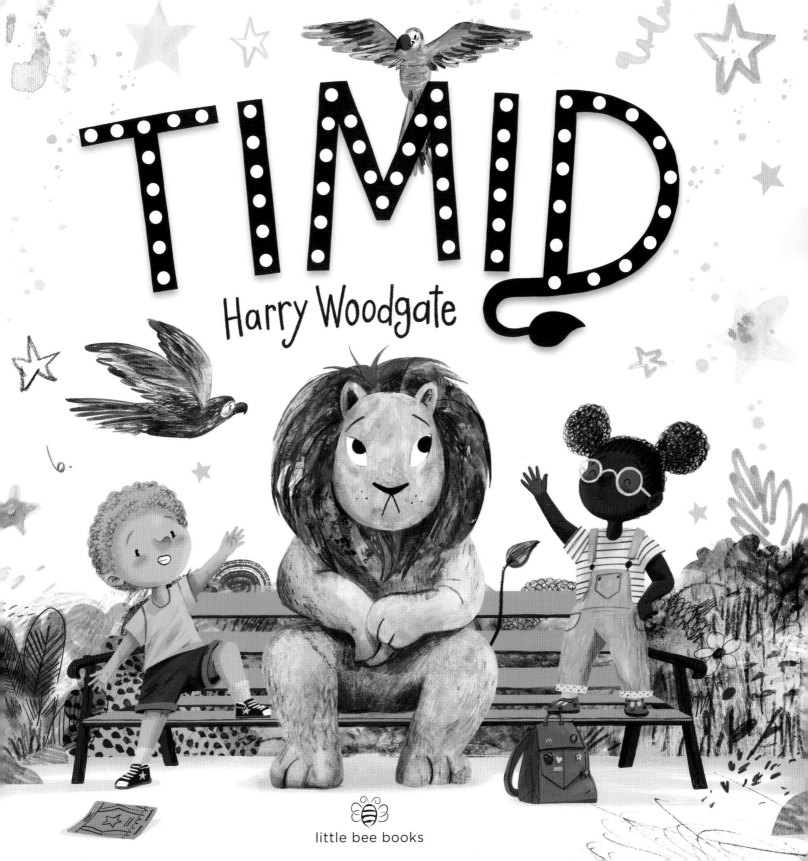

TIMID

Harry Woodgate

little bee books

There was nothing that Timmy loved more than performing.

They loved spinning around in sparkly costumes, speaking in silly voices, and singing along to songs that made their heart soar.

THEATRE
ADMIT·ONE
DOORS OPEN 7:00 PM

Hello! My name is: Timmy
My pronouns are: they/them

STAR OF THE WEEK

Here in their little room, they could make up all sorts of marvelous stories and become anyone they wanted to be.

Timmy dreamed of one day taking the stage
and sharing their stories with others.

There was just one small problem.

Well, actually,
it was a rather big one.

They were far too shy! Whenever they tried to talk to somebody new, a giant lion would appear out of nowhere and *ROAR* all their confidence away.

Timmy felt the lion's shadow all day. They couldn't focus on anything—

not science, not English,

not even gym class.

So, when Mr. Stevens told the class about the upcoming school play, Timmy didn't feel excited.

"I'd be too scared to perform anyway. What's the point when you're looming over me all the time?"

At lunch, Timmy watched the other kids play together.
"I wish I was brave like everyone else."

"Who are you talking to?" their classmate Nia asked.
"Do you have an imaginary friend? I do. Some people
say they're not real, but I know they are."

"He's . . . not really a friend,"
Timmy squeaked.

"Oh. That's a shame.
What's your not-a-friend's name?"

The lion roared.
Timmy wasn't quite sure
how to translate a roar.

"What are you going to be
in the school play?
I want to be a macaw.
I love their colors!" Nia said.

Timmy liked macaws too.
They reminded them of ballroom dancers and drag queens, but the words kept swirling around the tip of their tongue, always just out of reach.

"You're very shy, aren't you?
That's ok. I am, too.
Most of the time I sit inside and draw,
but Mr. Stevens said I should
play outside because it's sunny.

I want to make my own costume for the play, but . . .
I'm too scared to show my design to anyone."

Nia seemed so confident—how could she
be nervous just like Timmy?

Timmy mustered up all their bravery
and told Nia about the big, angry lion.

"That must be your not-a-friend! Let's make a plan.
If I show you my design and you help me make
an amazing costume, I'll help you tame your lion
and perform in the play. Deal?"

"If I help you rehearse, you can get used to performing in front of someone else—then it won't be as scary on the big day!" Nia suggested.

The lion let out an anxious grumble, but acting in front of Nia wasn't nearly as scary as performing for a big crowd.

Perhaps if they built up their confidence, they'd be able to perform after all!

Next, they set to work
crafting their costumes.

Timmy helped Nia carefully glue and stitch
all the different pieces together,
until finally they stood back
and looked at their creations. . . .

It was as if Nia had worked out
how to show what a song felt like—
all the calm, quiet moments
and the loud, energetic ones too!

"What do you think?"
Nia asked nervously.

"I think we look wonderful!"
Timmy said, proudly.

As the play got closer, Timmy and Nia tried
more and more ways to overcome their shyness.

"My brother says that meditation helps him
calm down if he's feeling anxious," said Nia.

"My mom writes encouraging notes
to stick up around the house," Timmy said.

"Whenever I'm preparing an assembly,
I think of the most embarrassing thing
that could happen, and then I act it out,"
suggested Mr. Stevens.

Timmy hadn't ever felt
this confident before.
In fact, they actually felt excited.

Soon enough, it was
opening night,
and the whole class
was getting ready
for the play to begin.

There was just one small problem.
Well, actually, it was a rather big one.
As they peeked out at the stage,
Timmy felt the familiar swish of a tail.
The lion was still there!

Suddenly, it all felt too much.

"The lion came back,"
Timmy said in between tears.
"There's no way I can
get back up on stage."

"Maybe the lion
is scared too," Nia said.
"Maybe he needs you
to tell him it's alright."

Come to think of it, the lion did look very worried.

"I've spent all this time trying to get rid of you,
when maybe we should have faced our fears together.
Perhaps you are my imaginary friend after all."

Now, Timmy was a fearless lion.
They were ready to go out
and put on a roaring show!